FETCH

For Kai & Rosa,
love Mum

Starring Kai, Rosa, the Chuckle Sisters and Frances

ORCHARD BOOKS
338 Euston Road, London NW1 3BH
Orchard Books Australia
Level 17/207 Kent Street, Sydney, NSW 2000

First published in 2012 by Orchard Books
First published in paperback in 2013

ISBN 978 1 40831 385 5

Text and illustrations © Jane Cabrera 2012

The right of Jane Cabrera to be identified as the author and illustrator of this work
has been asserted by her in accordance with the Copyright, Designs and Patents Act, 1988.

A CIP catalogue record for this book is available from the British Library.

1 3 5 7 9 10 8 6 4 2

Printed in China

Orchard Books is a division of Hachette Children's Books,
an Hachette UK company.
www.hachette.co.uk

FETCH

Jane Cabrera

ORCHARD

One cold, wet night, in a town not far from here, a little black dog slowly made his way through the dark streets.

He was tired.

He was hungry.

He was lost.

The next morning, Rosa spotted the small, shivering dog huddled next to the bins.

"You're so cold!" she said,
and she ran back to her house.
"Mum, MUM!" she called.

"Poor little thing," said Mum, "he's shivering. Let's bring him inside and get him warm."

Rosa dried the little dog and Mum put out some food and water. Then they made him a cosy bed in the corner.

"Mum, can we keep him?" Rosa asked.

"We'll see," answered her mother.

"Right now, it's time for school –
where's your bag?"

Suddenly, the little dog
bounded over to Rosa.

He had fetched her bag!

Later that day, he
fetched Mum's umbrella,

Baby's favourite rabbit
and Dad's slippers.

"I think I'll call you
Fetch!" giggled Rosa.
Fetch wagged his tail.

Soon, Fetch was helping all over town.

On **Mondays**, Fetch helped Mr Muffin at the newsstand, delivering newspapers and magazines. (But he refused to deliver Cat's World.)

On **Tuesdays**, Fetch helped Mr P at the Post Office. He licked stamps, fetched parcels and collected the dropped rubber bands for Mr P's giant rubber band ball.

On **Wednesdays**, Fetch helped at Miss Dolly's busy shop, fetching bags for the customers, and sometimes fetching things he wasn't supposed to!

On **Thursdays**, Fetch helped Mrs Peacock, fetching string and ribbon and delivering balloons to birthday parties.

On **Fridays**, Fetch helped
everyone clean and tidy.
Always wagging his tail, he fetched
buckets, brooms and brushes.

"What would we do without you?"
his friends asked.

On Saturdays and Sundays,
Fetch and Rosa went to the park.

They had fun throwing and
fetching a ball together all day long.

And, every evening, Fetch skippity-skipped
and wagged his tail all the way up to
the big house on the hill, where
his friend Lou-Lou lived.

He always fetched
her a special treat.

Then, one Monday, Fetch wasn't at the newsstand.

He wasn't at the Post Office on Tuesday . . .

POST OFFICE

POST OFFICE

. . . or at the busy shop on Wednesday, or with the balloons on Thursday . . .

. . . and, on Friday, the cleaning was no fun without him. His friends looked everywhere, but there was no sign of Fetch.

Rosa waited at the park all day Saturday
and most of Sunday, too. But Fetch
was nowhere to be seen.
Where was he?

Suddenly, there was an excited "Woof!"
There he was! And, for the first time ever,
he had fetched . . . nothing.

He ran back into the bushes
and came out with Lou-Lou by his side.
And this time he had fetched . . .

. . . a puppy! "

Fetch gently placed it at Rosa's feet.
Soon, he had fetched one, two,
three, four, five little puppies.
As Rosa hugged Fetch she told him,
"This is the BEST thing you've
ever fetched!"

The end